Izzy the INVENTOR

and the CURSE of DOOM

USBORNE QUICKLINKS

DISCOVER EXPERIMENTS LIKE THE ONES IZZY TRIES IN THIS BOOK
AND FIND OUT MORE ABOUT THE SCIENCE BEHIND THEM...

AT USBORNE QUICKLINKS WE HAVE PROVIDED LINKS
TO WEBSITES WHERE YOU CAN:

• Find out how to build a volcano and watch it erupt.

• Discover how to make tissue paper parachutes.

• See how simple ingredients can make fake snow –
perfect for your own snow creations.

• Find lots more experiments to try at home.

TO VISIT THESE SITES, GO TO USBORNE.COM/QUICKLINKS
AND TYPE IN THE KEYWORDS "IZZY AND THE CURSE OF
DOOM" OR SCAN THE QR CODE ON THIS PAGE.

PLEASE FOLLOW THE INTERNET SAFETY GUIDELINES
AT USBORNE QUICKLINKS.

CHILDREN SHOULD BE SUPERVISED ONLINE.

IZZY the INVENTOR

and the CURSE of DOOM

Zanna Davidson

ILLUSTRATED by ELISSA ELWICK

Contents

Meet Izzy

She wants to be the...

GREATEST INVENTOR

of ALL time.

Izzy always believed in **SCIENCE**, *not* magic. But then, one day, something unexpected happened. A fairy appeared in her bedroom, saying...

It is I, Rose Petal Twinkle-Toes, your Fairy Godmother.

The fairy gave Izzy a unicorn (which she hadn't asked for), sent her on a mission to Fairytale Land (which she didn't believe in) and told her to rescue Prince Charming from the Mountain of Doom.

Life, for Izzy, would **never** be the same again...

CHAPTER ONE
A Bad Start...

Izzy was having a lovely dream about a picnic with all her favourite scientists.

Einstein was there...

These are relatively good sandwiches.

Izzy was telling them about
her latest AMAZING inventions.
They all seemed very impressed.

But then Izzy heard someone, with a very tinkly voice, calling her name over and over.

The dream **VANISHED** and Izzy opened her eyes to see a fairy and a roly-poly unicorn had appeared beside her bed.

"There's a problem," said Fairy
Rose Petal.

"**A big problem**," added Henry
the Unicorn.

Fairytale Land is in trouble again and we need your help.

It's all because of BAD FAIRY BRENDA.

I was worried this was going to happen...

"Bad Fairy Brenda wasn't invited to Cinderella's wedding," said Fairy Rose Petal, "and now she's put a Curse of Doom on ALL fairy tales, starting with Sleeping Beauty. It will take more than a prince to wake her now..."

To break the curse, we have to find a way to make it SNOW in the FOREVER SUMMER MEADOWS...

...and for me to fly. But look at my wings!

"Can't you solve the problem with some *magic*?" asked Izzy.

"Only the Winter Pixies can make it snow," said Fairy Rose Petal. "And we're not asking *them*."

Henry gave a shudder. "The Winter Pixies are **AWFUL!**"

They make your nose go red...

turn the ground all slippy...

...and then laugh when you fall over.

"And we've tried making Henry fly," sighed Fairy Rose Petal, "but no amount of magic seems to work. So, Izzy, we need you and your **SCIENCE SKILLS**. You'll just have to come to *Fairytale Land* and save the day."

But I've got SCHOOL today!

It's only 6am. We'll have you back before school begins.

"There's no need to fuss," said Fairy Rose Petal, airily. "I'm sure you and Henry can fix this."

Here's a map. Good luck!

Then Fairy Rose Petal fluttered through the open window, leaving behind a trail of pink sparkles.

"Please help," begged Henry. "I don't want it to be *my* fault if Sleeping Beauty has to sleep for all eternity."

"Of course I'll help," said Izzy, giving Henry a hug. "Let me just get a few things."

Izzy started packing her **SCIENCE** bag.

I'll need ingredients for making fake snow...

My equipment...

Last of all, Izzy
packed her science
notebook, and
got dressed.

Then Izzy jumped onto
Henry's back...

Henry leaped out of the
window...

bounded through the garden...

...and sailed through the shimmery pink mist.

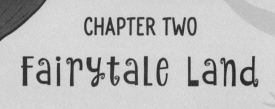

CHAPTER TWO
Fairytale Land

"Isn't it great to be back?" said Henry, doing a little twirl as they arrived in *Fairytale Land*.

"Yes..." said Izzy. "Although I don't think I've been to this part before. It doesn't exactly look **FRIENDLY**."

"Let's visit Sleeping Beauty's Castle first," Izzy went on. "I want to make sure she *is* asleep. You can never be too sure with Fairy Rose Petal. I'll check the map."

FAIRYTALE LAND

INEDIBLE FOREST

MOUNTAIN OF DOOM

FAIRY SPA

JACKIE'S BEANSTALK

BOTTOMLESS LAKE OF DESPAIR

HOME FOR RETIRED FAIRIES

HOME FOR RETIRED ELVES

OGRE BEAUTY PARLOUR

BOG OF INCREDIBLE STENCH

FAIRYTALE WOODS (WITH GOBLINS)

SLEEPING BEAUTY'S CASTLE

FROZEN WASTES
(HOME TO THE WICKED
WINTER PIXIES)

IMPENETRABLE THORNY FOREST

YET MORE
FAIRYTALE
WOODS

FOREVER SUMMER
MEADOWS

RUMPELSTILTSKIN'S HOUSE

FAIRYLAND FARM

SNOW WHITE'S
COTTAGE

"It says we need to be noble princes and have large axes," said Henry. "This could be tricky."

"Well, I think you're a **prince among unicorns**," said Izzy.

Henry blushed.

"I know!" said Henry. "I could try using my horn."

"Oh, look!" Izzy called. "Someone's already made a path."

"Oh, phew!" said Henry. "Onto my back, Izzy! We'll race like the wind!"

"**AT LAST**," said Izzy, when they reached the castle door. "We've made it!"

They went inside...

"It's a bit **CREEPY** here, isn't it?" said Henry.

"And the castle is **HUGE**," said Henry. "How are we ever going to find *Sleeping Beauty*?"

Izzy
and
Henry
climbed
the
twisty
stairs...

At the very top of the turret was a little room. And inside, lying on a sofa, was 𝒮𝓁𝑒𝑒𝓅𝒾𝓃𝑔 𝐵𝑒𝒶𝓊𝓉𝓎. She was fast asleep and snoring.

Very loudly.

They don't mention the snoring in the fairy tale...

zzzzzzzzzzzzzzz

"*Now* what?" asked Henry.
"Now we try and wake her," said Izzy.

But **nothing** seemed to work...

"Oh dear," said Henry. "She is definitely very, very, deeply asleep."

Before Izzy could reply, a prince came into the room, with a large cup of tea.

Oh, hello! I see you can't wake Sleeping Beauty either.

"I've been trying to wake her for *ages*," said the prince, "but nothing seems to be working."

"Oh no!" cried the prince, aghast. "If Sleeping Beauty doesn't wake up..."

...then I'm doomed!

"Don't worry," said Izzy. "I have a plan, Prince... Sorry, I just realized, I don't know your name?"

"It's Prince," said the prince.

"Prince what?" asked Izzy.

"Just Prince," insisted the prince.

"It can't just be Prince," said Izzy. "You must have *another* name."

"Okay, I'll tell you," said the prince. "But you musn't laugh. Do you promise you won't laugh?"

We promise we won't laugh.

It can't be worse than Charming.

It's Potato.

"Everyone laughs," sighed the prince. "Even worse is when they pronounce it POT-AAAH-TOE."

Oh that's terrible.

"Well, the good news, Prince Potato," said Henry, "is that Izzy here has been sent to wake Sleeping Beauty. Apparently, all we have to do, to break the curse, is make it snow in the Forever Summer Meadows, and for me to fly."

"**FLUTTER**?" said Prince Potato.
Then he turned to Izzy.

"I'm **99%** sure I can do this," said Izzy. "But it would be good to know...

...what happens if we fail and *Sleeping Beauty doesn't* wake?"

"Then the fairy tale will be **ruined**," said Prince Potato.

"Who wants to read that *Sleeping Beauty* just slept on and on? Think what that book would look like..."

And from that day forward, Sleeping Beauty slept on and on...

45

"**NO ONE** is going to read that fairy tale, are they?" demanded the prince. "And if no one reads my fairy tale, it won't just be the Mountain of Doom that's doomy. I'll be **doomed** too."

Why? What happens if no one reads your fairy tale?

Prince Potato of DOOM.

Shh! That's not something we talk about.

"I might as well tell you. You'll find out soon enough. I fade away, getting fainter and fainter until I COMPLETELY DISAPPEAR. NO MORE. GONE. KAPUT."

"It's okay," said Izzy. "I'm on the case. I'll work this out. I'm not IZZY the Inventor for nothing."

With those words, Izzy began leafing through her notebook. "Yes! Here we are..."

FAKE SNOW RECIPE

Ingredients

- Tray or bowl
- Cornflour
- Baking soda (also known as bicarbonate of soda)
- Water

- A squirt or two of shaving foam (optional)

Notes:

 This is a really easy experiment!

If the snow turns out too dry, you can just add a few more drops of water. Or if it's too runny, you add more baking soda and cornflour (in equal amounts).

"**Hooray!**" said the prince. "So all you need to do is make this mixture and then we'll be one step closer to breaking the curse."

We did it!

When it was ready, they all looked at the bowl of fake snow.

Henry and the prince danced a little jig together in celebration.

But at that moment, Bad Fairy Brenda zoomed into view. "So you've got some snow, have you?" she sneered. "But how are you going to make it look as if it's *actually* snowing? Didn't think of that, did you?"

Then, in a puff of black smoke, Brenda was **gone**.

"Oh no!" said the prince. "What are we going to do now?"

Look at me! My arms are starting to fade! And Henry STILL can't fly. I'm dooooooomed.

53

CHAPTER THREE
Rabbits to the Rescue

"We're not giving up *that* easily," said Izzy. "There's always a way. What we need now are some fairies."

They could fly around dropping our fake snow, and then it would look like it's snowing!

"It's the day of the Fairy Gathering!" explained Henry. "All the fairies mysteriously disappear for the day. No one knows where, but it must be **REALLY** important."

55

Just then came the sound of voices. A lot of voices.

Chill out, Izzy!

You're in a tizzy!

There's no need to fuss...

You can count on US!

Oh look! It's the Rhyming Rabbits.

What can we do...

...so we can help you?

"Well..." said Izzy, and she quickly explained the problem.

We'll fly high and low...

...and sprinkle your snow!

"Oh, thank you!" said Izzy. "That would be brilliant."

"We'll do it for the prince," chanted the rabbits. "He's making us wince!"

Look, there goes his nose!

Next up are his toes!

Oh woe, oh woe! I've lost my toes...

"Oh no," said the prince. "Now I'm rhyming *and* vanishing."

Izzy was busy handing out the fake snow. "Where has Brenda gone? She needs to see this!"

Brenda! Oh, Bad Fairy Brenda! Where are you?

Quick, Rhyming Rabbits! Go as fast as you can.

When **Bad Fairy Brenda** came back, she looked **FURIOUS**.

"We made it snow!" crowed the prince. "Now all we have to do is find a way for Henry to fly."

So take that, Brenda! You're hardly a SCARY FAIRY, are you?

Bad Fairy Brenda shook her wand and narrowed her eyes. Henry gulped.

"So you made it snow, did you, **little clever clogs**?" snapped Brenda. "Well, if you're so brilliant..."

...maybe I need to make it harder for you?

No!

Bring. It. On.

I declare that Sleeping Beauty shall not wake until...

"...Henry the **HOPELESS** Unicorn can fly and the **MOUNTAIN OF DOOM** erupts! So there."

You can't ADD to the curse!

Says who? And actually, in fairy tales, things always happen in threes.

62

"This isn't **FAIR**!" wailed poor Prince Potato.

"You should be *thanking* me," retorted Brenda. "It could be so much worse."

How? How could it be worse? I can see the ground through my feet.

You could be a frog!

"So long!" called Brenda, flying away again. "Good luck!"

"You really need to work on that evil laugh!" Prince Potato called after her.

Brenda turned back and tried again...

"**STILL** not impressed by your laugh," said the prince.

"Well, you'll have vanished soon, Prince *Pot-aaah-toe!*" cackled Brenda.

"It's not *Pot-aaah-toe*. It's *Pot-ay-toe!*" shouted the prince. But it was too late.

Brenda had GONE.

CHAPTER FOUR
The Mountain of DOOOOOOOM

"Oh dear," said Henry. "We seem to have made things **WORSE**."

Prince Potato looked sadly at where his arms had once been. But Izzy was determined. "I didn't know the **MOUNTAIN OF DOOM** was a volcano?" she said.

"It last erupted about a thousand years ago," said Prince Potato, glumly.

I bet you can make it erupt again!

Yes... I believe I can!

"What's more," Izzy went on excitedly, "the **MOUNTAIN OF DOOM** will make the perfect spot for Henry's first flight!"

"I'm not sure that sounds very safe?" said Henry.

Izzy wasn't listening. "I'll just pack up my equipment," she said, "and then we can go!"

It took them a long time to reach the **MOUNTAIN OF DOOM**, as Henry kept stopping for snacks. By the time they arrived, Prince Potato's legs were starting to go.

"Oh!" said Izzy, when they reached the very top of the mountain. "What are all these fairies doing here?"

We're having a day trip.

Hello, dear. We're from the Home for Retired Fairies.

That prince is in worse shape than us!

71

"We weren't invited to the Fairy Gathering," explained one of the fairies. "So we came here to cheer ourselves up."

"Well, we're here on an urgent mission," said Henry, proudly, "to break Bad Fairy Brenda's curse."

We've already made it snow in the Forever Summer Meadows.

Now we're going to make the Mountain of Doom explode!

"Actually, first of all," said Izzy, "I'm going to prepare your flying outfit, Henry. Then, as soon as we've got the volcano to erupt, you can jump off the mountain."

"You see," Izzy went on, "I can't *exactly* get you to fly, but I am going to make you glide. And for that, we need **HEIGHT!** Now, let me just check my science notebook. Yes! I know what to do..."

"Do you **REALLY** think this will work?" asked Prince Potato. "I'm not sure how much longer I've got left!"

"It'll be fine," said Izzy, breezily. "What about Henry?" said the prince. "He doesn't look very, er, **aerodynamic?**"

"He doesn't need to be," said Izzy. "We've got height, and a bit of wind. Hopefully that will waft us down to Sleeping Beauty's Castle."

Now you just wait here, Henry, and I'll start on the volcano.

How to make a volcano
(prepare for mess!)

Ingredients

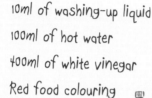

10ml of washing-up liquid

100ml of hot water

400ml of white vinegar

Red food colouring

Empty 2-litre plastic bottle

Baking soda slurry
— fill half a cup with
baking soda, and the
rest with water

Method

1. Combine the vinegar, water, washing-up liquid and 2 drops of food colouring in the empty 2-litre bottle.

2. Use a spoon to mix the baking soda and water in a cup, until it is all a liquid.

3. Eruption time! ... Pour the baking soda slurry into the bottle and step back!

Here we go! An excellent science experiment! And I think I've packed everything I need...

Izzy carefully measured all the ingredients and began mixing them together.

"Well, not *that* big," admitted Izzy, "but Brenda didn't say how big it had to be, did she?"

"No," said Prince Potato, "but Brenda is very picky."

"We can help," said the retired fairies. "Our magic isn't as powerful as it once was, so we couldn't conjure up an **explosion**."

But we can certainly make one bigger.

Really? That would be brilliant!

Izzy added the baking soda slurry.

The fairies
aimed their wands.

The mixture began to

froth and **bubble**

and then all of a **SUDDEN** the
bottle fell off the edge and...

The whole mountain began to shake as the mixture spurted up into the sky.

But then, the Mountain of Doom
began to rumble EVEN MORE.
Everyone started to

WOBBLE,

this way
and that.

"What's going on?" cried Henry. "This is starting to feel a bit TOO real."

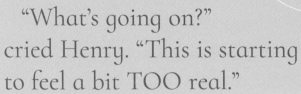

Maybe the magic was more powerful than we thought?

Then everyone gasped.

SOMETHING ELSE was beginning to emerge from the

MOUNTAIN OF DOOM.

It was horned and scaly. It had **HUGE** wings and was breathing fire.

Is that a... DRAGON?

"OOPS," said the retired fairies. "We forgot about her. She's been sleeping in the **MOUNTAIN OF DOOM** for years."

"In fact," said one of the fairies, "that's why it's called the **Mountain of Doom**, isn't it? Whoever wakes the dragon will be gobbled up."

The retired fairies rushed for the lift. "Sorry, dear," they called to Izzy. "You had better save yourselves. I'm afraid there's no room in the lift for us all."

"Goodbye," said the fairies, as the lift doors closed, "and good luck! You'll need it..."

CHAPTER FIVE
Henry's First Flight

Izzy jumped onto Henry's back. "Here goes!" she said. "It's time to fly!"

What was left of Prince Potato
floated onto Henry's back.

Jump,
Henry!

Henry looked down, his knees
wobbling. "Have I ever mentioned
that I don't like heights?"

Then he looked back at the
dragon, skulking towards them.
"Although, now I think about it,
dragons are even scarier."

Henry **shut** his eyes and **JUMPED!**

For a moment, he was gliding through the air. "This is amazing!" declared Prince Potato.

WHEEEE! Look at me! I'm flying! I'm really flying!

Maybe with a bit of help, but still...

I LOVE this! It's so much better than hacking through forests, looking for sleeping princesses...

Izzy looked back. "Oh no!
The dragon's coming after us!"
"She'll never catch us!" said
Henry, confidently.

Watch out
for that
beanstalk!

"Oops!" said Henry. "I think we might be **STUCK**."

"I'm going to cut us loose," said Izzy. "It's our only option. Otherwise the dragon will get us for sure."

"Now **FLAP** your wings, Henry," she cried. "See if you can fly!"

For a moment, it was as if time stood still for Henry.

Can I really do this?

No! I can't! I'm hopeless at everything, except dancing.

But I'm a unicorn, aren't I? And unicorns can fly!

Only my wings are so small. And we're so... GULP... high.

"You've got this!" said Prince Potato. "I know you can do this, Henry. We believe in you!"

And suddenly, Henry realized they were no longer falling.

"Um, Henry!" said Izzy.
"I don't know how to tell you
this, but..."
Henry looked
DOWN.

OH MY
GOODNESS!

"What do we do now?" said Henry. "Is this **THE END**? Death by deadly dragon?"

"I don't think the dragon is going to eat us," said Prince Potato.

"She's smiling at you," said the prince. "I think you've saved us after all, Henry. It must be because you're so pure of heart."

Me? Pure of heart?

Absolutely.

"In that case," said Henry, addressing the dragon, "would you mind taking us back to *Sleeping Beauty's Castle*?"

CHAPTER SIX
Lettuce &
Potato

The dragon did exactly
as Henry asked, and
flew them straight to
the castle.

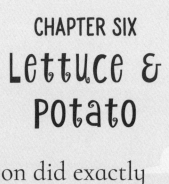

Just in
time.

"Thank you," said Henry. "That was very kind."

The dragon made a low, rumbling sound. Then she leaned forward and gave Henry a kiss.

Gosh.

Meanwhile, Prince Potato (what was left of him) hurried in through the window to find Sleeping Beauty.

"I must reach her before I completely disappear," he said, floating into the room.

As soon as he entered, Sleeping Beauty shot up from the sofa. And SCREAMED.

Aaaarrrgghhhh!

"Royal princess," said Prince Potato, "you have been asleep for a hundred years and a day but my arrival has broken the curse and now you are awake again."

Sleeping Beauty screamed even louder.

Aaaarrrgghhhh!

"Is this a nightmare?" she said.

"Why would it be a nightmare?" asked Prince Potato.

You don't have a body.

Yes, about that...

"My body should be coming back any minute now," said Prince Potato. "At least, I really hope so..."

"So it was you who broke my curse?" said Sleeping Beauty, smiling at him.

"It was I!" said Prince Potato, proudly.

And then he thought about it. "Well, I did have a bit of help from Henry and Izzy..."

"Maybe it wasn't really me who broke the curse after all," said Prince Potato, sadly. "All I did was slowly vanish."

"But you did hack through the **IMPENETRABLE THORNY FOREST** with your large axe," Henry pointed out.

"And," said Izzy, "you were very good-natured about turning invisible. You didn't complain nearly as much as I would have."

"And you were a HUGE help when the parachute got stuck. So encouraging," added Henry.

"Thank you!" said Prince Potato, smiling at Izzy and Henry.

I LOVE a group hug!

Me too.

Sleeping Beauty had started smiling too. "Did someone say **PARACHUTE?** I LOVE parachuting."

"You do?" said Izzy. "They never mention that in the fairy tale, either. I'm not sure how well my design really worked though..."

May I see it?

Of course!

"I have to say," said Sleeping Beauty, "I do prefer a glider. I have one that I made myself on the castle roof. Would you like to come and see it?"

"Yes please!" said the prince.

It's amazing!

Glider launch pad this way

"Of course you can come," said Sleeping Beauty. "But I don't even know your name."

"Ah!" said the prince. "It's... It's... It's... **Potato**."

"What a lovely name!" said Sleeping Beauty.

"Really?" said the prince. "You're not going to laugh? Or call me Pot-aaah-toe?"

"Of course not," said Sleeping Beauty.

And what's your name? I can't keep calling you 'Sleeping Beauty' if you're awake.

It's Lettuce.

Then Princess Lettuce and Prince Potato climbed aboard her glider and floated off into the sunset.

In a shower of sparkles, Bad Fairy Brenda appeared. She watched them go, a grim smile playing about her lips.

They overthrew my curse! But NEXT TIME no one will escape!

Henry and Izzy looked at each other. "You saved another fairy tale," said Henry. "And Prince Potato. And me."

"Actually," Izzy replied, "it was you who saved us all in the end, Henry. Because you're so pure of heart."

At that moment, the air began humming with fairies.

Goodness, you're all looking very... er... glamorous.

"Thank you, Izzy!" said one of the fairies. "You broke Brenda's curse. We couldn't have done it without you!"

"Well, we *could* have done," Fairy Rose Petal added, "but it was very important that we all attended the Fairy Gathering."

We had such a wonderful time!

"And what **EXACTLY** is this very important gathering?" asked Izzy. "Because it looks to me as if you've all spent the day getting your hair done."

"And painting our nails," said another fairy, giggling.

"Even fairies need a break sometimes," said Fairy Rose Petal. "And now I'd better send you back to your world, Izzy. School will be starting soon."

Goodbye, Izzy! Until next time!

When the sparkly mist cleared, Izzy saw she was back in her bedroom. Moments later, her dad came in.

"Izzy!" he cried. "What are you doing? It's time for breakfast."

You're not even dressed for school!

I, um, overslept! I'll be down in just a moment...

As soon as the door had closed, Izzy reached for her book of fairy tales.

"I just need to make sure everything really is okay in Fairytale Land!"

Izzy turned to 𝒮leeping ℬeauty...

Sleeping Beauty

The heroic Prince Potato (whose name shall not be laughed at) hacked through the thorns and woke Princess Lettuce. Then they flew off together into the sunset, in Lettuce's cleverly designed glider...

Sleeping Beauty

But Bad Fairy Brenda was NOT AMUSED. "I won't let a unicorn and a clever clogs get in the way of my curses like that. I will lock Henry the Unicorn in a tower for the REST OF HIS LIFE.

And the tower shall be guarded by a giant, a wolf and a talking harp..."

The End

Oh no! I have to get back to Fairytale Land and SAVE HENRY...

Here are some experiments from
Izzy's *science notebook*...

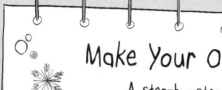

Make Your Own Snow
A step-by-step guide by Izzy

What you need:

- A tray or bowl
- 250g cornflour
- 1½ tablespoons of water
- 250g baking soda
  (also known as bicarbonate of soda)

Method

1. In a bowl, mix together equal amounts of cornflour and baking soda.

2. Add a very small amount of water into the bowl and mix together with your hands. Add a few more drops at a time.

3. Stop adding water once the mixture starts to hold its own shape, but crumbles when pressed — just like snow!

4. You can also try adding a squirt of shaving foam or hair conditioner that is white.

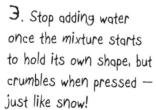

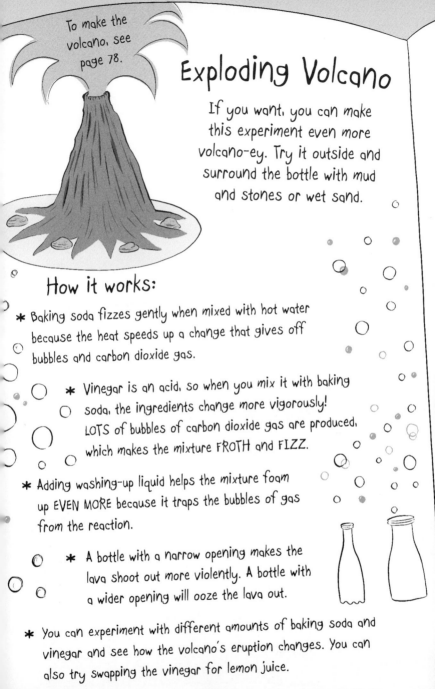

To make the volcano, see page 78.

Exploding Volcano

If you want, you can make this experiment even more volcano-ey. Try it outside and surround the bottle with mud and stones or wet sand.

How it works:

* Baking soda fizzes gently when mixed with hot water because the heat speeds up a change that gives off bubbles and carbon dioxide gas.

  * Vinegar is an acid, so when you mix it with baking soda, the ingredients change more vigorously! LOTS of bubbles of carbon dioxide gas are produced, which makes the mixture FROTH and FIZZ.

* Adding washing-up liquid helps the mixture foam up EVEN MORE because it traps the bubbles of gas from the reaction.

  * A bottle with a narrow opening makes the lava shoot out more violently. A bottle with a wider opening will ooze the lava out.

* You can experiment with different amounts of baking soda and vinegar and see how the volcano's eruption changes. You can also try swapping the vinegar for lemon juice.

125

Build Your Own Toy Parachute

A step-by-step guide
by Izzy

What you need:

- Tissue paper
- String • Scissors
- Sticky tape • Ruler
- A small plastic toy figure to be the parachutist, or some pipe cleaners.

What to do:

1. Take a piece of square tissue paper and lay it out on a flat surface.

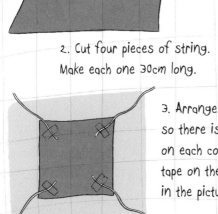

2. Cut four pieces of string. Make each one 30cm long.

3. Arrange the string so there is a piece on each corner, then tape on the string, as in the picture.

4. Pull the strings straight and tie all four ends together, about 5cm away from the loose ends.

5. Attach the loose ends of the string to the toy figure. If your figure is too light, add some modelling clay to make it heavier.

6. If you haven't got a small toy you could make one with pipe cleaners. Make a loop for the head, then bend the pipe cleaners to make arms and legs.

How it works:

When an object falls there are two main forces acting on it:

gravity
(a DOWNWARDS
force)

AND

air resistance
(an UPWARDS
force).

Without a parachute, your object would fall quickly, as gravity is greater than air resistance. But when the parachute opens, it increases the upwards force of the air resistance. This makes the parachutist fall more slowly.

* Try out different materials for your parachute. Which is the best material?

* A parachute can be circle-shaped or square-shaped. Try both and time them to see which falls faster!

SCIENCE SAFETY

ALWAYS TAKE EXTRA CARE WITH HOT OR SHARP THINGS
AND NEVER PUT ANYTHING IN YOUR MOUTH. IF AN
ACTIVITY INVOLVES DOING SOMETHING YOU MIGHT NOT
USUALLY DO, ASK YOUR GROWN-UP TO HELP YOU.

series designer: Brenda Cole
series editor: Lesley Sims
cover design by Freya Harrison
and Hannah Cobley
Digital manipulation by Nick Wakeford